I0530985

Frostbite

IVY GRANGER PSYCHIC DETECTIVE

Frostbite

E.J. STEVENS

Published by Sacred Oaks Press
Sacred Oaks, 221 Sacred Oaks Lane, Wells, Maine 04090

First Printing (trade paperback edition), July 2018

Copyright © E.J. Stevens 2017
All rights reserved

Stevens, E.J.
Frostbite/ E.J. Stevens

ISBN 978-1-946046-30-7 (trade pbk.)

Printed in the United States of America

PUBLISHER'S NOTE
This is a work of fiction. Names, characters, places, and
incidents either are the product of the author's imagination or
are used fictitiously, and any resemblance to actual persons,
living or dead, business establishments, events, or locales is
entirely coincidental.

The scanning, uploading and distribution of this book via the
Internet or via any other means without the permission of the
publisher is illegal and punishable by law. Please purchase
only authorized electronic editions, and do not participate in or
encourage electronic piracy of copyrighted materials. Your
support of the author's rights is appreciated.

Introduction

Welcome to Harborsmouth, where monsters walk the streets unseen by humans...except those with second sight.

Whether visiting our modern business district or exploring the cobblestone lanes of the Old Port quarter, please enjoy your stay. When you return home, do tell your friends about our wonderful city—just leave out any supernatural details.

Don't worry—most of our guests never experience anything unusual. Otherworlders, such as faeries, vampires, and ghouls, are quite adept at hiding within the shadows. Many are also skilled at erasing memories. You may wake in the night screaming, but you won't recall why. Be glad that you don't remember—you are one of the fortunate ones.

If you do encounter something unnatural, we recommend the services of Ivy Granger, Psychic Detective. Co-founder of Private Eye detective agency, Ivy Granger is a relatively new member of our small business community. Her offices can be found on Water Street, in the heart of the Old Port.

Miss Granger has a remarkable ability to receive visions by the act of touching an object. This skill is useful in her detective work, especially when locating lost items. Whether you are looking for a lost brooch or missing persons, no job is too small for Ivy Granger—and she could certainly use the business.

We can also provide, upon request, a list of highly skilled undertakers. If you are in need of their services, then we also kindly direct you to Harborsmouth Cemetery Realty. It's never too early to contact them, since we have a booming "housing" market. Demand is quite high for a local plot—there are always people *dying* for a place to stay.

FROSTBITE

"What a beautiful cat, Miss Granger."

I frowned, but let the comment slide. I didn't have any pets, not unless you counted the dust bunnies collecting beneath my desk.

Jess "Jinx" Braxton raised a questioning eyebrow, but I shrugged. I didn't have anything helpful to share with my rockabilly business partner. The frail woman tottering along at Jinx's elbow either needed new glasses or she was nuttier than weresquirrel poop.

Mrs. Boyd wouldn't be my first loony client. Working for a client who sees things that aren't really there is an occupational hazard when you advertise as the city's best (and only) psychic detective.

Who was I to judge? One of my special talents is the ability to see through glamour. A lot of supernatural creatures use glamour to hide in plain sight, and my gift cuts through the glitz and glitter of vampire compulsion and faerie magic. It's not as fun as it sounds. I've seen things no human should ever see.

Second sight is a blessing and a curse.

Monsters walk the streets of Harborsmouth. If it slinks, slithers, flies, or oozes, I've probably had the dubious pleasure of making its acquaintance. The fact that some of those things cross the street to avoid me hasn't escaped my notice. A detective's job is to take note of the little things, the small details that can break a case wide open, but having anthropomorphic snot treat you like you smelled worse than a troll fart could give a girl a complex. Some things are best to ignore or chalk up to sunny disposition.

I gave our client my best smile and waved a gloved hand at the seat in front of my desk. She flinched and latched onto Jinx's tattooed arm, huddling like a gryphon chick beneath its mother's wing. My partner shot me a warning glare and I toned down the charm.

"So, what can we help you with, Mrs. Boyd?" I asked, leaning back in my chair.

Best not to scare the client, at least not before she paid. Jinx reminded me of that often enough, and she kept the books. If she said we were in the red, then we were hemorrhaging our last pennies. Magic weapons and protective spells don't come cheap, and Jinx complains when we run out of food. So, I rested my gloved hands on the desk where my client could see them, adopted a relaxed pose, and tried not to let the woman's cat comment stir up painful memories of my childhood pet. Fluffy was dead and there was no sense living in the past. Surviving in the present was hard enough.

"Please, call me Maggie," she said, taking a seat.

Mrs. Boyd, Maggie, cast a nervous glance toward Jinx. I sighed, but nodded for Jinx to stick around. It looked like we'd be working this case together.

The fingers on my right hand reflexively went to my forearm, checking and double-checking the comforting presence of the silver-tipped iron blade hidden beneath my leather jacket. Something had our client spooked and Jinx was the people person in our little business venture, but having my partner leave the office set my teeth on edge. She was organized, great at keeping me on track, and sweet as cherry pie to our clients, but my partner had a knack for personal injury. We didn't call her Jinx for nothing.

"Okay, Maggie," I said. "How can we help?"

I held my breath, trying not to fidget in my chair. Maybe this would be an easy case, something completely mundane. Not every case was fraught with danger. Jinx might finally make it through a case without bumps and bruises.

So why were my insides being torn up by a pack of rabid vampire bats?

"It's my house," she said, waving her hands. Her cheeks flushed and her over-bright eyes darted between Jinx and me. "It's haunted."

That was doubtful. There are a lot of weird things that exist in Harborsmouth. I knew that more than most. But I'd never seen a ghost.

I put on my best poker face, leaned forward, and made a show of picking up a pen and flipping open my notepad.

"Can you describe this ghost?" I asked.

"Oh, the place is quite haunted," she said. "There's more than one ghost. I'm sure of it."

"And what makes you say that?" I asked.

"Furniture moving, moaning, groaning...that sort of thing," she said, blinking rapidly.

Jinx mouthed "pooka orgy?" from over Maggie's shoulder, and I had to stifle a giggle. My lip twitched, but I'd learned the hard way not to act like a crazy person in front of the clients, not until the check cleared.

"Have you noticed anything missing?" I asked, pen tapping a blank sheet of paper. "Spoons? Candleholders? Jewelry?"

"Nothing like that," she said, shaking her head.

Well, that ruled out Jinx's pooka orgy theory. I'd worked a few pooka infestations, and the supernatural rodents were notorious for stealing anything shiny that wasn't nailed down with iron. The only thing the bacchanalian critters liked more than an orgy was thievery.

"You're sure?" I asked.

"No, the only thing I've lost is weight," she said. "Which is strange since I'm hungry all the time. Not that I'm complaining. I was carrying around more than a few extra pounds before moving here last month."

That was hard to believe. The woman was gaunt to the point of emaciation. I narrowed my eyes and turned my head, trying to see through any lingering glamour. Most of the time, my gift works on its own, whether I want it to or not, but sometimes it needs a nudge.

"You moved here recently?" I asked, making a show of taking notes.

Sneaking up on the truth works in tricky cases, but all I saw in my peripheral vision was a frail woman in need of a sandwich. Something strange was going on here, and I had a bad feeling that I'd have to use my psychic gift before this case was solved.

You see, I'm twice cursed. Not only do I have the gift of second sight, a gift I'd happily return, but I also get visions when my skin touches certain objects. During a vision, I slip into a memory and experience events through the eyes of whoever left a psychic impression behind. The trouble is, it takes strong emotions to leave behind a psychic impression, and most things that make a person feel that deeply are painful or terrifying. Experiencing that much fear isn't healthy, and there was a very real risk of losing my sense of self, becoming trapped in someone else's nightmare, but sometimes it was the only way to solve a case.

Psychometry was a dangerous gift, but it paid the bills.

"Were there any belongings left behind by the previous owners?" I asked, chest tightening. "Or any rooms that weren't fully renovated before you moved in?"

"Oh, yes," Maggie said. "I've barely touched a thing. I had big plans for the place, but I haven't felt up to a big D.I.Y. project yet. I just haven't had the energy. And there are the ghosts to think of. Will you look into the matter? I know it's a strange thing to investigate, but when I asked around, everyone said that you're the one to handle weird...unusual cases."

I gritted my teeth, but nodded. I'd always been an outcast, a weirdo. Screaming about monsters and slipping into unwanted visions had led to a lonely childhood until I'd met Jinx.

"I'll take the case, but I need to investigate your house, go through some of the previous owner's old things," I said.

"Of course," she said, clutching her handbag to her chest. "Is today too soon? It's just...I haven't been sleeping. At least, I don't remember the last time I slept."

"No problem," I said. "Jinx has the address?"

She nodded, and I pushed away from the desk and stood. We had an active case and I didn't want to waste time, but it would be foolish to run off without a plan. My eyes flicked to the wall clock.

"Expect us around two o'clock," I said. "You're welcome to go out while we investigate. Just leave the door unlocked."

That gave us over an hour to come up with a plan and stuff my pockets with weapons and protective charms. I'd like more time, but the woman was visibly shaken. Whatever had invaded her home was drawing her energy in some way. She was practically fading out of existence as we spoke.

"Thank you, Miss Granger," she said, already standing and scurrying toward the door. "And don't worry about me being home. I retired just before moving to Harborsmouth, and I hardly ever leave the house."

Maggie Boyd walked out onto the streets of the Old Port Quarter, and I frowned. She was so sickly and rail thin, I'd mistaken her for an elderly lady, but the woman was only recently retired and more likely in her sixties. So much for my keen observational skills.

"Buck up," Jinx said with a wink. "So what if we have a reputation for taking on whacked cases? I say bring it on, the stranger the better. Weird is the new cool."

That was easy for her to say. Jinx hadn't seen the creatures that roamed our city, stalking humans as prey and ensnaring them in a deceitful web of pestilential lies and poisonous bargains.

I shrugged and opened the desk drawer where I kept my stash of hardcore protection charms. We were once again heading into unknown territory with no clue of what we were up against. Jinx could go on thinking a weird case like this was cool, but I listened to my gut, and right now my insides were churning into painful knots as my stomach tried to climb out my ear.

I was good at finding the truth, but I had a nagging suspicion that Maggie's house wouldn't reveal its secrets without a fight.

*****

Maggie Boyd's new digs were in a neighborhood to the north of the Old Port Quarter, wedged between the slums of Joysen Hill and the gentrification of the Quarter. There was a lower ratio of bars to homes here, but the streets weren't entirely residential. I would have missed the dead-end lane entirely if it wasn't for the kids using the sign for target practice. Their ammunition was broken chunks of pavement, but I gave them a smile with too many teeth, and they scattered.

We made it partway down the alley before the gang tags stopped and the brick buildings ended, replaced by a truck graveyard on one side of the street and a weed-strewn lot on the other. At the end of the lane, stood a simple house that had seen better days.

The house was a basic single-story Cape with faded clapboards that might have been red at one time, but now gave the appearance of flaking rust. A chain-link fence and the backside of a warehouse rose behind the structure, leaving the house in deep shadow. The alley was also dark, making the yard in front of the house the only sunny spot. Weeds, grass, and tangled vines thrived in the patch of sunlight.

"She has her own secret garden, cool," Jinx said with a grin.

"So did Miss Havisham," I muttered.

I eyed our exits before approaching the house. Maggie hadn't lived here long, but it was still surprising that the exterior and grounds were this rundown. If I didn't know better, I'd have guessed the place abandoned for decades.

I stepped gingerly over bits of debris, boots crunching on gravel as I made my way slowly down the footpath. The gate was gone, rotten away or scavenged for firewood, but my skin tingled as I passed beyond the dilapidated wooden fence and into Maggie's dooryard. A chill ran up my spine and I spun on my heel, but whatever I'd sensed, I was too late.

Jinx let out a startled cry, arms windmilling in an attempt to stay upright, but her platform sandals weren't helping. She reached out a hand, and I jerked away. It was a reflex born of years of negative visions, but I knew I'd screwed up.

As if Jinx's look of hurt and resignation wasn't bad enough, I overcorrected and landed on all fours. Warm wet grass slid inside the gap between my sleeve and glove, as if the ground was hungrily running its many tongues along my wrist, tasting my skin.

I shuddered, yanking my hand away and rapidly climbed to my feet. I'd had a run-in with Hunger Grass on a previous case and it hadn't gone well. In fact, the case had gone to Hell in a handbasket of woven rusty razorblades.

I rubbed gloved hands against my pants, and shuddered. Backpedaling, I glanced left and right, but nobody was trying to eat our faces off. It was just Jinx and me.

"What the heck just happened?" Jinx asked, frowning. "You get a vision?"

"Not a vision," I said, voice shaking. I swallowed hard, attention shifting to the house as I stepped back onto the path. "Our client ever mention an unexplained hunger or neighborhood pets going rabid?"

"No," she said, brow wrinkling.

"You sure?" I asked.

"I'd have remembered pets foaming at the freaking mouth," she said. "What gives?"

The correct question was, what takes? Hunger Grass was nasty stuff. Most people who step on a patch of the stuff end up changed and not for the better. First you lose your sense of right and wrong. Then you lose everything and everyone you ever loved.

I was immune to the stuff, but I had no idea why and even less interest in finding out. I'd hoped to never encounter that kind of magic again. No such luck.

"Our client has a patch of Hunger Grass in her front yard," I said, glancing at Jinx. "You know what that means."

She did. Jinx went pale, eyes widening.

"Oh shit," she said.

Oh shit was right. Hunger Grass was extremely dangerous. Most faerie magic is. But it takes more than just magic to create the slavering circle of weeds.

Something bad happened here, really bad. Like famine or a hard Maine winter driving a family to cannibalism bad.

"You think there are actually ghosts in there?" she said. I had to hand it to my partner. Her face was ashen, but she didn't run away. "The ghosts of eaten people."

"I don't know," I said, squaring my shoulders. "But we're going to find out."

The crunch of gravel beneath my boots punctuated my words and I tried not to think about trudging over bones picked clean of flesh. I barely twitched when Jinx rapped on the door, announcing our arrival.

We didn't have to wait long. The door swung open and Maggie stood there, eyes appearing sunken in the dim light. Had she touched the Hunger Grass? Was she infected with its magic?

"Please, come in," she said. "I'll be in the kitchen if you need anything. Don't leave without coming back for tea. The kettle's almost ready."

I stepped inside the house, a polite refusal on my lips, but gasped. The shabby living room fell away, revealing a horror so great I was at a loss for words.

This is not at all what I expected.

"What do you see?" Jinx asked, sidling up to me as our host passed through what I assumed was the kitchen door. "Looks normal enough."

"You don't want to know," I said, swallowing bile.

The walls were slabs of pulsating meat and the floor was sticky beneath my combat boots. I winced at the moist fetid air that hung heavy with the distinctive stench of a slaughterhouse. Fear and blood permeated every fleshy crevice, but over the underlying terror loomed a hunger that threatened to devour us whole.

"Jinx, go outside," I said, voice hard.

"Outside with the creeptastic Hunger Grass?" she asked.

She had a point.

"Fine, but keep close to me," I said, lowering my voice. "Stay away from the walls and don't touch anything. Assume that nothing in this house is what it seems."

"That's not very reassuring," she muttered.

"Good," I said, palming my knife. "If you're scared, we might just get out of this alive."

"What about Maggie?" Jinx asked.

A tapping came from the kitchen, and I stilled. Tap, tap-tap, tap. There was an agonizing pause before the tapping began anew. As much as I'd love to run screaming from this bizarre charnel house, we had a case to solve and a client to rescue.

"We're going to accept that cup of tea and find out what the hell is going on in this house," I said.

"And if it's a trap?" she whispered.

"We'll cross that bridge when we come to it," I said.

I just hoped that if we did encounter a bridge, it wasn't made of oozing muscle tissue.

On my signal, Jinx pushed open the kitchen door. At least, she swore it was a wooden door. If we made it out of here alive, I'd need a gallon of brain bleach to scrub that orifice from memory.

I gasped, staggering forward, but abruptly froze as my eyes darted back and forth from Maggie to the corpse wearing her clothes. Corpse might be too kind a word. The body was missing parts and had been gnawed on by more than rats.

That wasn't the scariest thing in the room, not by a long shot.

I'd located the source of the tapping. Two children huddled on the floor, their knobby knees and the jut of their collar bones painful to witness. They leaned into each other in a one-armed embrace, teeth chattering against a cold I couldn't feel.

"You can see them, can't you?" Maggie asked, voice hopeful and eyes pleading.

"She doesn't mean the bones on the floor, does she?" Jinx whispered from where she stood at my back.

"No, Jinx," I said. "But those bones are important. I'd put money on it."

In fact, the corpse huddled around the children's tiny forms, giving them comfort, even in death.

"Can you help them?" Maggie asked.

I glanced from Maggie to the body on the floor, and took a deep breath. I lifted my eyes to the children, turning my head to use the full strength of my second sight. The children flickered, but I caught a glimpse of rows of needle-like teeth, too many teeth for their gaunt faces.

Tap, tap-tap, tap. The chattering continued, and I winced.

"What...what did you do?" I asked.

"What any good mother would do, or so I thought," she said. "I eased their suffering. I kept them alive. I didn't know what would happen to them."

I was going to ask what she meant, but my mind finally caught up with what my eyes were seeing. They didn't have mouths ringed red and sticky from berry preserves and the youngest wasn't holding a doll to her chest. The little girl stroked a clump of her mother's hair.

"You were starving," I said.

Maggie nodded, eyes never leaving her children.

"They were excited for the snow, at first," she said. "It came late that year, but it more than made up for its tardiness. The winter was never-ending. And for them, it never will end. Not without your help."

"What can I do?" I asked.

"Tell them that they are good children," she said. "They did what they were told. They mustn't suffer for my evil act."

I frowned, but stepped forward and crouched down, careful not to touch the body at my feet. Being cannibalized was one vision I sure as hell didn't want to get sucked into.

"Ivy, what are you doing?" Jinx hissed.

What was I doing? I looked at the children, using my second sight to see every detail. Their teeth wasn't the only unnatural anomaly. Vein-like tendrils connected the children to the fleshy cabinets and gelatinous floor.

"Maggie's children are tethered here," I said, replying to Jinx.

I glanced up at Maggie, searching her face for clues. Her eyes were wide, but she leaned forward.

"Is that why they couldn't move on?" she asked. "Can you...?"

"I'm no expert," I said, cutting her off. "But from what I see, this house is feeding on the children's suffering. If I'm right, it might not like us removing its food supply."

"Is this a bad time to mention I'm not really dressed to battle a haunted house that feeds on the suffering of dead kids?" Jinx asked.

"Wishing you'd taken your chances with the Hunger Grass?" I asked.

"Hell, yes," she said. "But you're not leaving, are you?"

"Hell, no," I said.

"Fine, but, for the record, I'm totally cool with you losing your weirdo street cred," she said.

"What happened to the stranger the better?" I asked.

"Our client is dead, the house is alive, and there's grass in the yard with the ability to create ravenous wendigos," she said. "That's what happened."

I'd been watching the children while Jinx rambled. They didn't respond to Maggie or Jinx, but I could have sworn their eyes slid to me more than once. Maybe my second sight allowed some creatures to see me more clearly.

"My name is Ivy Granger," I said. "What's yours?"

They didn't reply, but both children turned their heads my way, unblinking. A low growling rose from their stomachs, and they stared at me with a feral gleam in their eyes. At least I had their attention.

Fear slithered along my spine and my glance darted around the room. Did Maggie invite us here to bring her children peace or dinner? I had to try to rescue the kids no matter my client's motives.

"I'm a friend of your mom's," I said.

Walls spasmed and red tears ran in rivulets down the children's cheeks.

"Ivy, did you feel that?" Jinx asked.

"Stay there and don't move unless I say so," I said.

Predators chase their prey. And these two stopped being innocent children long ago.

"Your mom is here and she loves you very much," I said. "You've been very good, but she needs you to do one more very hard thing."

"B-b-bad," the boy said.

"No, you're not," I said.

"H-h-hungry," the little girl moaned.

"You don't have to ever be hungry again," I said. "You can move on and be with your mom again."

I had no idea if what I said was true, but words have a magic of their own and there were strong energies in this house.

I tapped into my own sense of emptiness at losing a parent, a hole in the pit of my stomach and an ache in my chest that would never go away. I channeled a child's yearning for their parents and told the ghost children what they needed to hear.

They were good. They were loved. They were going home.

The more I talked the more convinced I was that I could save them. And just like that, a door opened and the children turned to face my client.

"Mommy?"

"Take my hand," Maggie said, reaching for her children. "We're going home."

The room shuddered, and Jinx lost her balance, but I kept my eyes on the children and the veins that tethered them to the house.

"We were bad," the girl said.

"No, my beautiful precious boy and girl," Maggie said. "You did exactly what your foolish mother asked of you. Can you forgive me?"

They ran to her, and as they reached the end of their fleshy chains, I sliced the veins with my blade. The knife was silver-tipped iron and sprinkled with holy water. I had no idea what the house was, but the veins blackened and withered, retracting with lightning speed.

Maggie mouthed "thank you" over the children's heads and stepped through the glowing door.

I heard her voice through the light, calling out in a cheerful voice.

"Come on, Fluffy," she said. "Time to go home."

Something brushed my leg and purring filled my ears. Then it moved away and the door snapped shut.

My ears popped and Jinx frowned.

"Was that a cat?" she asked.

I blinked away tears.

"I don't know, but I don't think we'll be getting paid for this job," I said.

Jinx looked around the dusty kitchen and groaned. The house was once again a mundane structure, the only oddities were the three bodies resting in each other's arms.

"We're never going to see a dime," Jinx said, staggering to the door.

The light was painfully bright, but I tilted my head to the sky and shrugged.

It's hard to pay the bills when you're dead. But if you die in a city filled with random faerie magic and have Ivy Granger on the case, you sure as Hell can settle your debts.

Did you enjoy Frostbite?

If you enjoyed this short story and would like to read more from the Ivy Granger series, please write a review. Writing a review is one of the best ways that you can show your support for the book, series, and author.

Thank you.

Ivy Granger Psychic Detective Box Set

Want to read more of Ivy's adventures?

The Ivy Granger Psychic Detective Box Set includes the novels
SHADOW SIGHT, GHOST LIGHT, and BURNING BRIGHT
for one low price.

Demons, ghosts, vampires, and necromancers—Ivy dodges the
city's deadliest villains while solving its darkest cases. Will she
save the day or die trying?

Order now to keep reading the Ivy Granger series.

Don't miss these books set in the world of Ivy Granger.

Ivy Granger, Psychic Detective Series

Shadow Sight
Welcome to Harborsmouth, where monsters walk the streets unseen by humans...except those with second sight, like Ivy Granger.

Blood and Mistletoe: An Ivy Granger Novella
Holidays are worse than a full moon for making people crazy. In Harborsmouth, where many of the residents are undead vampires or monstrous fae, the combination may prove deadly.

Ghost Light
Ivy Granger is back, gathering clues in the darkest shadows of downtown Harborsmouth. With a vengeful lamia on the city streets, reports of specters walking Harborsmouth cemeteries, and an angry mob of faerie clients at her office door, it's bound to be a long night.

Club Nexus: An Ivy Granger Novella
A demon, an Unseelie faerie, a human, and a vampire walk into a bar...

Burning Bright
Burning down the house...

Birthright
Being a faerie princess isn't all it's cracked up to be...

Hound's Bite
Ivy Granger thought she left the worst of Mab's creations behind when she escaped Faerie. She thought wrong.

Tales from Harborsmouth
A collection of Ivy Granger short stories and novellas.

Hunters' Guild Series

Hunting in Bruges
The only thing worse than being a Hunter in the fae-ridden city of Harborsmouth, is hunting vampires in Bruges.

Coming soon to the world of Ivy Granger

Blood Rite

Ivy Granger psychic detective takes on a simple grave robbing case, but in Harborsmouth nothing is ever simple when dealing with the dead.

Warning: This book features grave robbing, an abandoned amusement park, necromancy, and zombie clowns.

Watertight

When Torn is accused of murdering a local mermaid, Ivy Granger is plunged into the deep end of water fae politics.

With her psychic gifts and newfound wisp powers, locating Torn's alibi should be simple. Too bad a deadly enemy with a score to settle is lurking in Harborsmouth's darkest waters.

Ivy Granger might be in over her head. Even with the help of her kelpie king fiance, Ivy only has until the next high tide to prove Torn's innocence. With the clock counting down and the bodies piling up, Ivy better hope she finds an alibi that's watertight.

Dressed in White

Something old, something new, something borrowed, and something blue...

On the eve of Jinx and Ivy's double wedding, a sinister figure is terrorizing Harborsmouth.

When reports of a homicidal jilted bride threaten their wedding plans, Ivy and Forneus set out to put a stop to the string of heinous acts. What they discover might just send the faerie and demon straight to Hell, and set Ivy on a path to rectify more than one evil deed.

Will Ivy tie the knot with her kelpie king, or will she be saying "I do" to the king of Hell? Her father's curse is on the line, and lives hang in the balance. No pressure.

Also by E.J. Stevens

Ivy Granger, Psychic Detective
Urban Fantasy Series

Frostbite
Shadow Sight
Blood and Mistletoe
Ghost Light
Club Nexus
Burning Bright
Birthright
Hound's Bite
Tales from Harborsmouth
Ivy Granger Psychic Detective Box Set is Now Available.

Hunters' Guild
Urban Fantasy Series

Hunting in Bruges

Spirit Guide
Young Adult Series

She Smells the Dead
Spirit Storm
Legend of Witchtrot Road
Brush with Death
The Pirate Curse
Spirit Guide: The Complete Series is Now Available.

Dark Poetry Collections

From the Shadows
Shadows of Myth and Legend

Ebooks, Trade Paperbacks, Audiobooks

Ivy Granger Psychic Detective novels and novellas are available in ebook, trade paperback, and audio. Look for the Whispersync for Voice symbol for special Audible and Kindle discounts.
Visit EJStevensAuthor.com to listen to free audiobook samples, interviews with the narrators, and more.

Get Lost in Translations

Ivy Granger books are available worldwide in multiple languages.
Visit EJStevensAuthor.com to learn more and get lost in translations.

Freebies

Visit the Freebies Page at EJStevensAuthor.com for free audiobook samples, Ivy Granger ringtones, wallpapers, and more.
Want a free book and access to ARCs, exclusive news, and giveaways?
Sign up for E.J.'s newsletter.

About the Author

E.J. Stevens is the bestselling, award-winning author of the IVY GRANGER, PSYCHIC DETECTIVE urban fantasy series, the SPIRIT GUIDE young adult series, the HUNTERS' GUILD urban fantasy series, and the upcoming WHITECHAPEL PARANORMAL SOCIETY Victorian Gothic horror series. She is known for filling pages with quirky characters, bloodsucking vampires, psychotic faeries, and snarky, kick-butt heroines. Her novels are available worldwide in multiple languages.

When E.J. isn't at her writing desk, she enjoys dancing along seaside cliffs, singing in graveyards, and sleeping in faerie circles. E.J. currently resides in a magical forest on the coast of Maine where she finds daily inspiration for her writing.

Stay connected at www.EJStevensAuthor.com.

www.ingramcontent.com/pod-product-compliance
Lightning Source LLC
Chambersburg PA
CBHW071230130626
46555CB00004B/1917